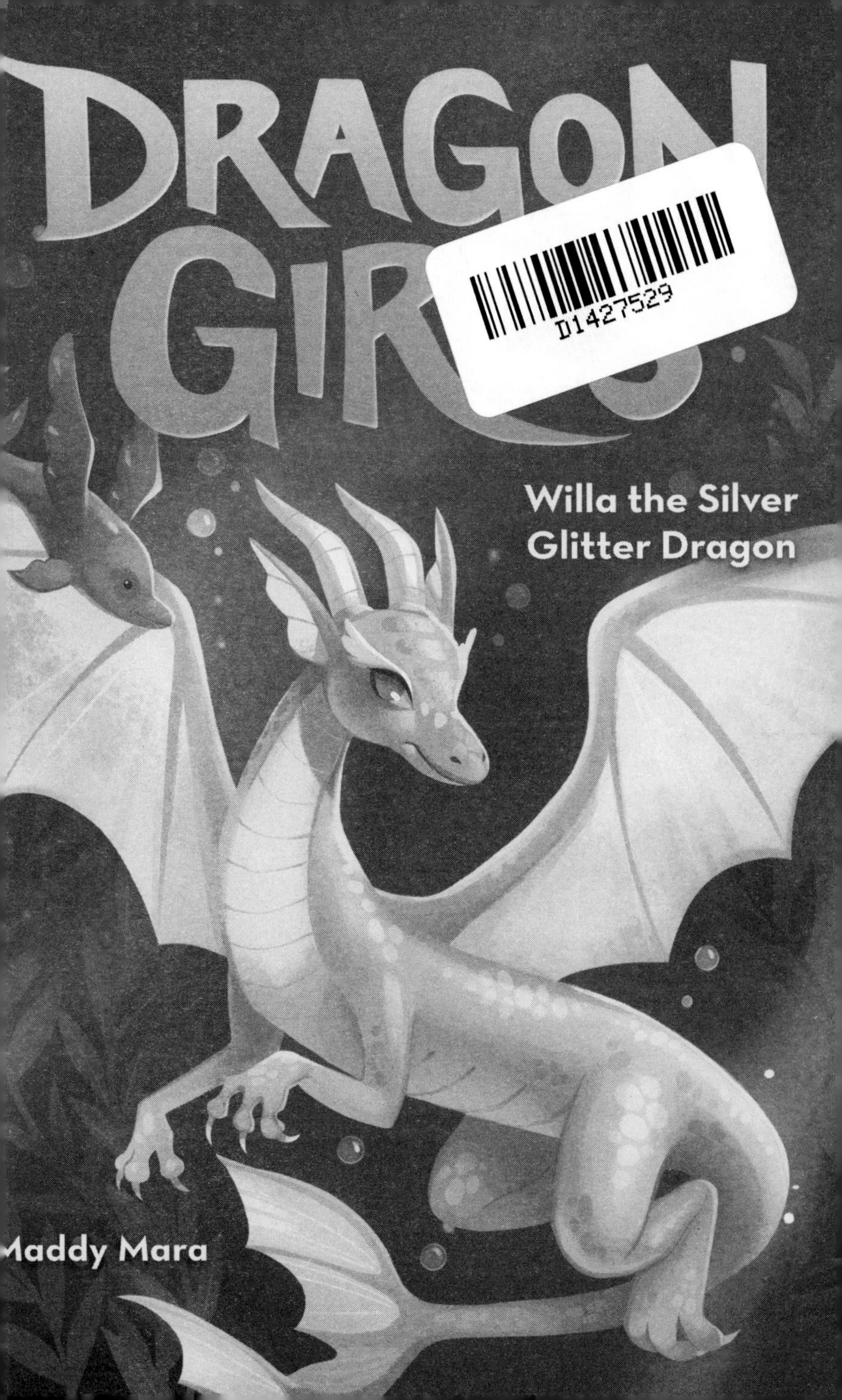
DRAGON
GIR
Willa the Silver
Glitter Dragon
Maddy Mara

DRAGON GIRLS

Willa the Silver Glitter Dragon

by Maddy Mara

SCHOLASTIC

Published in the UK by Scholastic, 2022
Euston House, 24 Eversholt Street, London, NW1 1DB
Scholastic Ireland, 89E Lagan Road, Dublin Industrial Estate,
Glasnevin, Dublin, D11 HP5F

First published in the US by Scholastic Inc, 2021

Text © Maddy Mara, 2022
Illustrations by Thais Damião © Scholastic Inc., 2021

The right of Maddy Mara and Thais Damião to be identified
as the author and illustrator of this work has been asserted by
them under the Copyright, Designs and Patents Act 1988.

ISBN 978 0702 31100 0

A CIP catalogue record for this book is available from the British Library.

Printed by CPI Group (UK) Ltd, Croydon, CRO 4YY
Paper made from wood grown in sustainable forests and other controlled sources.

3 5 7 9 10 8 6 4 2

This is a work of fiction. Names, characters, places, incidents and dialogues
are products of the author's imagination or are used fictitiously.
Any resemblance to actual people, living or dead, events or locales
is entirely coincidental.

www.scholastic.co.uk

Book design by Stephanie Yang

For Madeleine and Asmara – and every other girl working on her roar

1

Willa stood at the edge of the local indoor pool, her towel wrapped around her shoulders. Beams of sunlight fell through the windows above and danced on the water's surface.

The other kids from Willa's swimming lesson had all hurried off to the changing rooms. But Willa stood gazing into the rippling water, thinking about all the amazing things that had happened to her recently. Only a few days ago, Willa's life had been perfectly normal. She had been a regular girl who loved swimming, diving and hanging out with her friends.

But that was before she had discovered the Magic Forest. When Willa was in the Magic Forest, she was anything but a typical girl. There, she and her friends turned into Dragon Girls! As Dragon Girls, they could fly, had incredible strength, and best of all, they could roar the most powerful and glittering roars!

Through the open window, Willa heard the wind pick up. She listened carefully. To anyone else, it might just sound like a breeze rustling the leaves. But Willa heard something more. The wind carried a special message, just for her. This was a message she had been waiting for ever since she got back from the Magic Forest.

Magic Forest, Magic Forest, come explore...

"Willa, are you coming to get changed?" called Nancy, the swim coach. "The lesson is over, you know!"

Willa smiled. "Yes, I know. Can I just do one more dive?"

"Sure," Nancy agreed. "But be quick. The next class starts soon!"

Just then, Nancy's phone rang. Willa's heart thumped. This was her chance! She knew time moved differently in the Magic Forest.

She could spend an entire day there, but when she returned, only a second would have passed.

While Nancy was distracted, Willa dropped her towel and returned to the water's edge. A beam of sunlight suddenly appeared, illuminating a small white seashell sitting on the bottom of the pool. The shell was shaped like a fan and was flecked with silver.

Willa felt drawn to the shell like a magnet. She had seen it the first time she was called to the Magic Forest. She knew it was no ordinary shell – it was her travel charm. She loved the way it fit perfectly into the palm of her hand, and how it was always warm to the touch.

Now its reappearance must mean it was time to return to the forest.

Magic Forest, Magic Forest, come explore...

The magical words were getting louder now. Willa knew she had to hurry. She curled her toes around the edge of the pool and stood up straight. She loved the way her body felt like an arrow, arcing through the sky before slicing into the water.

True, her dives were still a bit wonky sometimes, but she was getting better and better. Willa raised her arms above her head.

Magic Forest, Magic Forest, come explore.

"Magic Forest, Magic Forest, hear my roar!" Willa finished, her voice echoing around the pool area.

Taking a huge gulp of air, Willa dived into the water.

On land, Willa wasn't all that fast or agile. But when she was underwater ... well, that was a different story! When she was swimming, Willa could move at top speed and hold her breath longer than anyone. She could also do all kinds of somersaults and tumbles and handstands.

But there was no time for tricks right now.

Willa focused on the shell lying below her on

the pool's floor. The sunlight made the shell

glimmer like it was on fire. As she got closer,

Willa stretched out her hand and wrapped her

fingers around the shell. Warmth spread up

her arm. Her insides tingled with excitement.

She was going to the Magic Forest again!

As Willa swam back up to the surface, still holding the shell, things around her began to change. The blue tiles of the pool faded away. In their place appeared the long leaves of river plants, waving gently back and forth. Rocks emerged, faintly at first, and then more solidly. Tiny jewel-like fish passed her, changing colours like a rippling rainbow as they flicked their tails.

Willa grinned in delight. Underwater was such a magical place.

And this water was very special indeed. Willa felt like she could hold her breath for

ever! She kicked her legs and shot ahead with incredible speed. She had never felt so strong before.

As she neared the surface, a gleaming, silver-skinned dolphin swam over and gently nudged Willa with its nose. Willa had the feeling the dolphin was saying hello.

Willa burst through the water's surface and took a big, sweet gulp of air. She looked around. The pool centre had completely disappeared. Willa was now in the middle of a shimmering lake, surrounded on all sides by a splendid forest.

Not just any forest, she reminded herself with a shiver. *The Magic Forest!*

2

Willa took a deep breath to calm her excitement. She knew that the pool turning into a glittering lake wasn't the only thing that had changed.

She raised the hand that was holding the shell up above the water. Her normal girl hand was gone. Instead, she saw a silver paw. As she watched, the shell began to shimmer and fade away. Willa wasn't worried. She knew that it would reappear when she needed it.

Excitedly, Willa looked down at her reflection in the smooth surface of the lake. Gone was her usual light brown hair and the spray of freckles across her nose. She had become a majestic silver dragon with sparkling grey-green eyes!

Willa laughed, and a puff of glittery smoke rose into the air. She was a Dragon Girl, and not just any Dragon Girl. She was a Glitter Dragon Girl! Willa had changed into dragon form before, but it felt just as thrilling every time.

As Willa admired her dragon-y self and gave a little roar to clear her throat, she heard a tinkling splash of water behind her. She turned just in time to see a very strange sight: the silver dolphin she'd seen in the water had leapt into the air.

Now, Willa loved watching nature shows

with her dad, so she often saw dolphins jumping high into the air. But she also knew that dolphins then dived back into the water.

But this dolphin wasn't doing that. Instead, it was doing loops in the air, over and over, like an acrobat training for the circus.

"Amazing! How can you do that?" exclaimed Willa.

She was NOT expecting the creature to answer her, but it did all the same. "I go where you go," the dolphin said in a funny, squeaky voice. "Underwater. In the air. Whenever you need me, I'll be there."

Willa knew that dolphins were smart and playful. But this was on a whole new level!

Willa gave a great underwater flap of her wings and rose up out of the water and into the sky. She'd never done that before and it felt wonderful! Glittery drops of water rained down from her long tail and strong paws. It was so good to be flying again.

And sure enough, the little dolphin zoomed up into the sky beside her, leaving a silvery trail of stars in its wake. When Willa did a mid-air somersault, the dolphin was right there doing one too. It reminded Willa of when her swim team trained together, everyone focused on the same moves.

"What's your name?" Willa asked the magical creature.

"Delphina," replied the dolphin, hovering in mid-air and giving Willa a formal bow of introduction. "That was fun, but now we must hurry. The Tree Queen is waiting for you."

This time it was Willa's stomach that did a somersault. Of course, she had been called to the Magic Forest for a reason!

"Are Naomi and Azmina already there?"

asked Willa, following Delphina as she zoomed ahead.

Naomi was one of Willa's oldest friends. They had met on the very first day of nursery and had been friends ever since. Azmina was the new girl who'd arrived at their school just this week. As soon as Willa saw Azmina, she knew they'd become friends.

But more than all that, Naomi and Azmina were also Glitter Dragons!

They had been summoned because the Magic Forest needed their help. The evil Shadow Sprites were gathering strength, trying to turn the forest into a place of constant gloom. It was up to the Glitter Dragon

Girls to help stop them. They had already completed one quest, but Willa knew that there was still work to be done.

"They've just arrived," squeaked Delphina. "I know a short cut. Follow me."

With a twitch of her tail, she sped off, tiny stars streaming behind her.

Willa was getting better and better at flying, but all the same it was hard to keep up with Delphina. It was lucky that she shone like polished metal, or Willa might have lost sight of her darting through the treetops.

Down below, Willa could see a wide and fast-flowing river. It was a glorious deep turquoise colour. Except ... hang on! In some places the river wasn't turquoise at all, but a horrible murky grey. As Willa watched, she could see the greyness was spreading through the water like curls of ink.

A coldness gripped Willa's chest. *Shadow Sprites*, she thought darkly.

Delphina seemed to sense her thoughts. "The Shadow Sprites are spreading through the water now, draining it of its goodness," she said. "The word in the forest is that they are working for the Shadow Queen."

"The Shadow Queen?" Willa frowned. "Is she that powerful?"

"A long time ago, she controlled the whole forest," explained Delphina. "Oh, she was a cruel leader. Lots of animals think she's trying to take over again, using the Shadow Sprites."

Willa did not like the sound of this Shadow Queen.

Finally, Willa caught sight of the glade where the Tree Queen lived. The Tree Queen watched over the Magic Forest and kept it safe. It was she who had called on the Glitter Dragons when the Shadow Sprites first began causing trouble.

As always, the air around the glade shimmered like it does on a hot day. But it wasn't hot. The shimmering was a special force field that protected the glade and everything – or everyone – inside it. Only those who wanted to help the Tree Queen were able to pass through.

Willa sighed with relief. She was almost there. The Tree Queen would know what to do about the sprites spoiling the river. She zoomed down below a low-hanging branch...and then, quite suddenly, she became stuck. She couldn't fly!

Don't panic! Willa told herself, but it was hard to fight the feeling. She couldn't move her wings. Maybe her wings were caught in the branches of the tree?

But when Willa looked, she saw something that nearly made her heart stop. Shadowy finger-like shapes were wrapped around the

tips of her wings, holding her. She shook them off. But almost instantly, more came, snaking around her wings and her legs too.

When she looked up into the tree's canopy, Willa saw more shadows coming down the branches towards her.

They made soft, whispery sounds. As they got closer, Willa saw their cold eyes. With a jolt, she realized she could hear words too.

Hopeless Dragon Girl... Can't fly as well as the

others... Loses everything...

The words seemed to seep into her, making her feel cold and worried. She shivered.

"Delphina!" she called through chattering teeth. "Where are you?"

"I'm right here. Don't worry," called Delphina.

Willa saw the dolphin flying towards her through the trees.

Willa was very glad to see her. "I can't move!"

"Hold still," commanded the dolphin, opening her mouth to show a set of very shiny, sharp teeth. "I'll have you free in a moment."

She flashed around Willa, nipping at the

shadows and tearing them away. They hissed angrily at the dolphin, but a few moments later, Willa was free … and tumbling towards the river below!

"Don't forget to flap your wings!" called Delphina.

But it was too late. Willa only had time to flip herself around and dive into the river.

As soon as she was in the water, Willa felt better. She wasn't a hopeless dragon! And maybe her flying wasn't the best, but that was OK. Willa felt at home in the water. Bubbles tickled her sides and she saw Delphina next to her, a wide grin on her snout and strange squeaky noises emerging from her mouth.

"Are you laughing at me?" demanded Willa.

"Maybe a little," admitted Delphina. "That was a pretty crazy-looking dive!"

"Definitely not my best. But I had just been attacked by Shadow Sprites!" Willa laughed.

In the cool water, she could feel her strength returning.

"Don't get too comfy," warned Delphina in a low voice. "There are even more shadows underwater than on land."

As she spoke, Willa saw a grey, see-through shape slither past.

"Let's fly the rest of the way," Willa said.

Delphina nodded. "The air is safer right now."

They burst back out of the water, showering

silver droplets everywhere. Willa was very glad to see the shimmering barrier of the glade up ahead. She felt like she'd had an adventure already, and the quest hadn't even begun!

Willa and Delphina landed near the shimmering air.

"I'm not coming into the glade," said Delphina. "But I'm never far away." With a flutter of her tail, she sent silver stars flying as she swished away.

Willa turned towards the glade's protective

force field. She took a big breath and stepped into it. The air pushed past her, warm and a tiny bit tingly. A moment later, Willa was through the force field and safe within the glade. She closed her eyes and breathed in the sweet smell of flowers and fruit.

She loved this place. All of the Magic Forest was incredible, of course, but there was something extra special about the glade. Somehow it always felt like the forest's heart.

"Uh, Willa?" said a voice. "Did you just fall asleep?"

"Maybe she's power-napping," said another voice.

Willa opened her eyes to see a rainbow

dragon peering at her curiously. Behind her was a golden dragon, laughing and sending little puffs of sparkling glitter into the air.

"Hi, Naomi! Hi, Azmina!" Willa grinned. "I'm not napping. I'm just really, really happy to be here. And to see you two, of course."

"Yeah, I always close my eyes when I'm happy to see someone," teased Naomi.

"Well, I'm pleased to see the three of you," said a warm, familiar voice.

Willa turned to see the stately tree in the centre of the glade transforming into the Tree Queen. Willa thought the queen was very beautiful. Her long wavy hair flowed around her face and across her mossy green gown.

But Willa couldn't help noticing that the queen looked a little tired. Were her arms thinner than usual? And her big brown eyes weren't quite so sparkly.

"Excuse me, Tree Queen, are you feeling OK?" she asked anxiously.

The Tree Queen smiled at Willa, but her smile was not as wide and bright as usual. "I am feeling better now that my Glitter Dragons are here," she said. "But it is true that I am not as strong as usual. The Shadow Sprites are still at work, you see."

"I thought we were safe in the glade." Naomi frowned.

"Everything within the glade is safe,"

confirmed the Tree Queen, "but my roots go deep into the earth and draw water from an underground river. And the Shadow Sprites are attacking the water."

Willa thought about the strange inky swirls she'd seen in the river and shuddered. She remembered what Delphina had said. "Is it true that they work for the Shadow Queen?"

The others looked at her curiously, but the Tree Queen just nodded. "She has been quiet for a very long time. But she is gathering strength."

Willa, Azmina and Naomi exchanged worried looks.

The Tree Queen stretched out one of her long branch arms, from which hung a tiny apple. It was no bigger than an acorn. As the Dragon Girls watched, the apple rapidly began to swell until it was a giant silver fruit – much bigger than an apple in the normal world.

The Tree Queen had grown a magic apple when they had last visited. But that time it had been gold.

"Look into the apple," said the queen in her soft, rustling voice.

The Dragon Girls leaned in and gazed at the shiny fruit. Slowly, images began to play like a film across the apple's surface. Willa felt like she was flying above the river again, although now she was much closer to the water. She had already seen the grey swirls wriggling through the water, leaving ashy trails behind them. But Willa was still shocked when they appeared in the bright turquoise water.

Even worse, the plants growing along the edge of the river seemed to be turning grey too. The Dragon Girls saw the river lead into the mouth of a huge cave, just before the images faded from the apple's surface.

"That cave is where the river starts to flow underground," explained the Tree Queen. "It flows directly under the glade, which is why I am not as strong as usual. The shadow water doesn't have the same minerals in it."

It was awful to think the Tree Queen might be losing power.

"Is there a potion that will help?" asked Willa.

Last time they had collected three rare ingredients to make a potion that super-charged their roars. That, in turn, had given the

Glitter Dragons the strength to overcome the Shadow Sprites.

"Yes, there is a potion," said the Tree Queen. "But the ingredients will be even more difficult to collect than last time."

"We'll find them," said Azmina firmly.

Willa smiled. Azmina was always so confident that they could do anything. The good thing was her confidence was infectious!

"What are the ingredients?" Willa asked.

The Tree Queen drew in a deep breath. It looked like it was a lot of effort for her to speak. And when she did, her voice was dry and crackly. "The first ingredient is a perfect egg from the Worrying Waterfall Bird," said the Tree Queen. "Follow the river and you will find it."

Willa felt herself relax. An egg didn't seem too complicated.

"The second ingredient is a single tear from a sea-donkey," the Tree Queen continued.

Hmmm... now that was definitely trickier. What even *was* a sea-donkey? Willa supposed it was a bit like a seahorse. But how could you gather a tear underwater?

The Tree Queen fell silent for a moment, like she needed to catch her breath. Willa didn't want to rush her, but she also knew that they were running out of time.

"And the third thing?" Willa asked politely.

The Tree Queen sighed and swayed her branches from side to side. "I am not entirely sure," she admitted. "My mind is not so clear today. It's something from somewhere very deep. And it's invisible."

"Invisible?" repeated Willa. She really hoped she'd misheard the Tree Queen. Finding something invisible was surely an impossible task!

But the queen nodded, her wavy hair falling across her serious face. "Yes, invisible. But you will know it when you see it."

"Or don't see it," muttered Naomi.

Willa could tell that Naomi was as puzzled as she was. Azmina was the only one who still looked confident. Willa was glad she was on the team.

"Hold out your paw, Willa," instructed the Tree Queen.

Willa did as she asked, and the queen let the apple drop.

As Willa caught the magical fruit, she felt nerves crash over her. "Um, last time Azmina took care of the apple."

"But this time the apple is silver," replied the queen. "And you are the Silver Glitter Dragon. It's your task to take care of it."

"Here, you'll need this to carry the apple," said Azmina kindly, taking off the soft bag she had worn on their last quest.

Willa looked at the others dubiously. "Don't you think Azmina should look after it again?" she said. "I might lose it or something."

She was thinking about the Shadow Sprites' whispers. What if they were right?

The Tree Queen smiled. "I believe in you, Willa. You should too."

Willa *really* hoped the Tree Queen was right!

The bag had looked golden when Azmina was wearing it. But as Willa put it on, it changed colour until it blended with her silvery tones. Willa slipped the apple inside. The bulge of the apple almost completely disappeared. And the bag was so light, Willa couldn't even

43

tell she was wearing it. She wished her school bag worked the same way!

Willa could see Naomi and Azmina watching her. She was nervous about being in charge of the apple, but she felt excited too.

Willa flapped her wings, sending silver glitter fluttering around her. "OK, let's go!" she called. "We'll follow the river until we find the waterfall."

Together, the three Glitter Dragons rose through the shimmering air and up above the treetops, their glitter settling on the glade's force field like twinkling snow.

Clouds began to gather, and it soon started to rain. But Willa had always liked the rain.

The big, silvery drops tinkled out strange melodies and kept her cool as they sped along.

When Willa had first tried flying, she'd found it very hard. She kept crashing into things! Then she discovered that if she imagined she were *swimming* through the air, it was easier. She especially loved diving through the sky, adding fancy twists as she whooshed down.

It was like jumping from the highest diving board at the pool.

But the best part about flying, Willa decided, was that Naomi and Azmina were there with her. Azmina had started making up a silly song as she flew along.

She had a really nice voice, rich and strong. Hearing her sing made Willa feel less worried about the quest ahead of them. Then Naomi joined in with the singing too. Naomi was a terrible singer, but she didn't care. She sang as loudly as she could until Azmina had to stop because she was laughing so hard.

Willa grinned at her friends. It was good to be one of the Dragon Girls!

But when Willa looked down, her good spirits dropped. Below them stretched the river, and it had even more grey swirls than before.

Azmina and Naomi noticed the murky water too. Azmina's usually bright smile faded.

Naomi stopped singing. "We'd better hurry!"

Soon Willa could hear falling water. It was getting louder and louder. And sure enough, when she looked up the river, she could see magnificent turquoise water spilling over the cliff and crashing on to the rocks below.

"The waterfall!" yelled Willa. "The bird we're looking for must live nearby."

"Nice work!" Azmina yelled back.

Together, the Dragon Girls swooped down

towards the waterfall.
They hovered in
front of the tumbling
water, the bright drops
spraying into the air.
It was very loud!

Willa was gazing at
the sheets of falling water when she spotted
something: "There's a cave back there!" she
called to the others. She'd always loved stories
about secret caves hidden behind waterfalls.
"Maybe that's where the Worrying Waterfall
Bird lives."

"How will we fly through all that water?"
asked Naomi. "Won't it crush us?"

"I bet we can slip around the side of the waterfall. We'll hardly even get wet," said Willa.

Azmina looked relieved. "I'm not wild about water – especially crashing, cold water! I like being warm and dry."

"We'll go together," decided Willa.

She led the way to the side of the waterfall. Sure enough, the water arched out from the cliff, leaving just enough space for the dragons to get through.

A curious light radiated from the cave.

"The cave is glowing!" said Naomi in awe as they gathered on the other side.

As they crept in, they soon found out why!

Balanced on rocks around the cave were

very big, very bright silver eggs. Some rested on ledges along the sides of the cave. Others were attached to the tree roots dangling from the roof. All the eggs twinkled like stars.

"They're so beautiful!" breathed Willa.

"Do you think so? Really? You *truly* think they're beautiful?" came a worried voice from the back of the cave. A large silver-feathered bird hurried towards them. "I sometimes *think* I lay the nicest eggs in the forest. But then I worry that's rude to all the other birds."

The bird talked on and on. This was definitely the Worrying Waterfall Bird!

When the bird finally stopped talking (just to take a breath), Willa jumped in. "Excuse

me, but have you noticed that the waterfall is changing colour?"

The bird flung up her wings. This was a whole new topic to worry about. "Yes! It's terrible! The water isn't what it used to be. I was just telling—"

"That's why we're here!" Willa interrupted as politely as she could. If she let this bird keep talking, they would never complete their quest.

"It's a problem throughout the Magic Forest," she explained. "We Glitter Dragons are making a potion to fix it. But we need one of your eggs. Could you spare us one?"

There were so many eggs in the cave, surely one fewer wouldn't matter. But then again, would such a worrywart be willing to give one away?

"Of course!" said the Worrying Waterfall Bird. The Dragon Girls exchanged relieved smiles. "Anything to help. Which one would you like?"

Willa looked around. The Tree Queen had said the egg needed to be perfect. But all the eggs looked the same to her.

"Maybe that one?" she asked, pointing to a nearby egg.

The bird rushed over and wrapped her wings protectively around the egg. "Oh, not this one! It's my favourite."

"How about this one?" suggested Azmina from the other side of the cave.

The bird immediately rushed over there. "Not that one! It's too pretty!"

"This one, then?" asked Naomi, picking up an egg nearby.

But the bird quickly snatched it out of Naomi's paw.

She couldn't give up that one, or the next

one, or indeed any egg that they suggested. They were all too wonderful to part with.

"Well, which one *can* we have?" asked Naomi, exasperated.

The bird looked at her precious eggs, thinking. Then she darted to the back of the cave. She returned with an egg in her beak and placed it carefully at Willa's feet. "This one."

It was much smaller than the other eggs. Instead of being silver all over, it was speckled with glittery dots. The Dragon Girls huddled together.

"We can't use it," whispered Naomi. "The Tree Queen said the egg had to be perfect. This one obviously isn't."

Azmina nodded. "We have to ask the bird to give us one of the others."

Willa picked up the egg. It fit exactly into her paw. The speckles sent silvery points of light across the cave's wall.

"This egg might not seem perfect to everyone," declared Willa, "but it's perfect to me. It's not too big, and it sparkles like I do."

The egg sparkled even brighter after she said that. The other two Dragon Girls nodded.

"You're right," said Naomi. "Put like that, it *is* perfect."

The bird hopped over, looking as worried as ever. "It is a lovely egg, isn't it? Perhaps I shouldn't—"

Willa quickly pulled out the magic apple. She wanted to get the egg in there before the bird changed her mind! But because she was in such a hurry, the egg slipped from her paw and fell into the apple and ... cracked.

"Nooo," groaned Willa, closing her eyes. She couldn't believe it. The very first ingredient and she'd already messed up!

"Don't worry, Willa," said Azmina excitedly. "I think it was *meant* to break. Look!"

Willa opened her eyes. A mist wafted up from the magic apple, filled with tiny shimmering stars. At the bottom of the apple lay a perfect silver egg yolk. The two halves of the eggshell quickly dissolved into a shiny powder. A moment later, the powder disappeared into the mixture inside the apple too.

Azmina was right. The egg was *meant* to break. They had completed the first step of the quest!

"OK! What's the next ingredient?" asked Naomi.

"A tear from a sea-donkey." Willa shrugged.
"Whatever *that* is."

"There's a sea-donkey family that lives not
far from here," said the Worrying Waterfall
Bird, stroking one of her eggs.

"Great!" said Azmina, ready to get going.

"But he might not be very helpful," said the bird.

"He doesn't need to be helpful," Naomi pointed out. "He just needs to cry."

"How do we find him?" Willa asked the bird, who was now scurrying around the cave, rearranging her eggs.

"Oh, that's easy," she said. "Just slide down the waterfall."

Willa felt a shiver of excitement. Sliding down the waterfall sounded like a lot of fun. Naomi clearly felt the same way. "Let's go!" she said, flapping her wings.

But Azmina was frowning. "Are you OK?" Willa asked.

Azmina nodded. "It's just, I'm not great at holding my breath."

"That's one thing even I wouldn't worry about," called the bird, dashing past with an egg under each wing. "Most dragons can breathe underwater for ages."

Naomi smiled at Azmina. "Hear that? If even a worry bird is telling you not to worry, you'll be fine."

Azmina nodded, but she didn't look completely convinced.

Willa put a wing around her. "We'll do it together, OK? We Glitter Dragons are a team."

Azmina nodded. "Thanks. And I guess I have flown into a volcano. Sliding down a waterfall can't be more difficult than that, right?"

"Exactly." Willa grinned, really hoping that was true.

~

Thanking the bird, the Glitter Dragons flew out of the cave and around to the front of the waterfall. It seemed even more powerful than before. Down below, the water churned fiercely.

In the "normal" world, there was no way Willa would slide down that waterfall. Much too dangerous! *But we are Glitter Dragons here in the Magic Forest, so everything is different,* Willa reminded herself.

She saw Azmina looking nervously at the

raging water. "Let's slide together," Willa suggested.

"Great idea," said Naomi. "Azmina, you go in the middle."

They flew to the top of the waterfall.

"On the count of three, let's slide!" roared Willa over the noise of the water. "One, two, three ... SLIDE!"

Whooshing down the waterfall was like riding on the fastest, splashiest waterslide.

"Whoo! This is fun!" yelled Azmina.

Willa grinned. She was glad Azmina was enjoying it. "Get ready to dive!" she roared as they plummeted down. Together, the Dragon

Girls took big breaths as they flipped around and dived nose-first into the river.

Below the surface, the water had a delicate blue light to it. But right away Willa saw shadowy shapes moving like eels through the water. Wherever the shapes wriggled, the water turned a murky grey.

Underwater, Willa could hear their whispering even more clearly than she had in the forest. *You'll never finish this quest. You don't have what it takes.*

The words made Willa feel like she was losing her sparkle.

"We have to hurry," she said. Hang on, she could talk and breathe underwater! Willa had always dreamed of being a mermaid.

"Would you mind getting out of the way?" asked a tired voice, pulling Willa out of her daydream. "I'm picking up my kids from school. You'll make me late."

Willa turned to see a very strange-looking

creature. It had tall, pointy ears, a horselike nose, and the curly tail and round stomach of a seahorse.

"You're a sea-donkey!" Willa gasped. "Just who we're looking for! We're on a quest, and we need your help."

"I don't have time for quests," the stressed-out little creature said, sighing. "The shadow water is confusing me. I keep getting lost! If I'm not at school when the bell rings, my kids will flip. Then the whole afternoon is a mess."

"We're here to fix the water," explained Willa. She had a brain wave. "I know, we could give you a lift!"

The sea-donkey dad looked hopeful. "Really?

That would save me! Like I always say to the kids, we sea-donkeys are smarter than sea-horses. But between us, I admit we're not as fast."

"Hop on my back!" said Willa.

The sea-donkey promptly did so, smiling

broadly. "This is great! The kids are going to be stoked when I turn up on a Glitter Dragon!"

The sea-donkey dad pointed out the way and they all headed off. Willa found it easy to glide through the water, even with the sea-donkey on her back.

The sea-donkey seemed much more relaxed now. He even started whistling as they sped along.

"Uh, Willa?" muttered Naomi, swimming up beside her. "We kind of need the sea-donkey to be sad, not happy. We have to collect a tear, remember?"

Willa had been thinking the same thing. But making the sea-donkey upset seemed mean, especially now that he was in such a good mood.

"You know, there's a mollusc at my kids' school who's going to college soon," said the sea-donkey suddenly.

"That's nice," said Willa, not sure why the sea-donkey was telling her this.

"Yup, she got a *scallop-ship*!" said the sea-donkey, braying with laughter.

Naomi groaned. "So it's not just human dads who tell bad jokes?"

"I think they're funny," Azmina chuckled. "And look! He's nearly crying with laughter."

"Azmina, you're a genius! I bet a happy tear will work even better than a sad one," whispered Willa. "Quick, think of all the dad jokes you know."

"Hey, Mr Sea-Donkey!" said Azmina. "What do you call a crayfish with a messy room?"

The sea-donkey looked over at Azmina. "What?"

"A slobster!" Azmina said, and the sea-donkey collapsed into fits of giggles on Willa's back.

"How did the oysters get to the hospital?" asked Naomi.

"Ooh, I know this one!" chortled the sea-donkey. "In a *clam-bulance*."

Willa tried to think of a joke. The perfect one hit her. "What do you call a fish with no 'eye'?"

"I know! I know!" yelled the sea-donkey, slapping his side in mirth. "You call it a ... you call it a—" He was laughing so hard he could hardly get the words out. "A FSSSSHHHH!"

And then something very strange happened. As the sea-donkey roared with laughter, tiny, sparkling droplets began spouting from his eyes.

"What's happening?" gasped Naomi. "Is he OK?"

A group of smaller sea donkeys swam over, each with a tiny shell school bag on their back. "Don't worry. Dad always cries like that when he's laughing really hard," one of them said.

"Those droplets are tears? Grab one!" Willa

called to Azmina and Naomi. But the tears weren't easy to catch. They kept sliding out of reach.

"All that laughing has used up my air," Azmina said. "I have to surface."

"Me too," admitted Naomi, starting to swim up. "We'll come back down in a minute, OK?"

But Willa knew that would be too late. She

had to catch a tear now! When a sparkling teardrop floated past, Willa opened her mouth and took a big mouthful of water. She had trapped the tiny tear in her mouth! Quickly, she began to swim up towards the surface behind Azmina and Naomi.

"Bye, Dragon Girls!" called the sea-donkey, gathering his chattering kids around him. "Thanks for the lift. And good luck with your quest!"

6

Willa kept her mouth firmly shut as she swam

back up to the surface. She did not want to lose

the precious sea-donkey tear she had trapped

in there.

She was feeling good. They already had two

out of three ingredients for the potion! Sure,

the last one was going to be the hardest, but

right then Willa felt sure they would find that one too. The Glitter Dragon Girls could do anything!

But before she reached the surface, Willa saw something strange coming towards her. It looked like a storm cloud, billowing and expanding in the water.

Willa frowned. *An underwater storm?*

As the cloud moved closer, Willa's stomach lurched as she realized what it was. *Shadow Sprites*... and more of them than she'd ever seen!

The shadowy mass swirled around and around, creating a kind of tornado. Willa watched in horror as anything that came near the whirlpool was sucked into its spinning darkness.

Azmina and Naomi were up ahead. It was clear that they hadn't seen the approaching danger. But Willa couldn't risk calling out in case the sea-donkey tear escaped from her mouth. The swirling shadows got closer and closer to her friends, draining the colour from the bright water as they went.

If Willa didn't do something, Azmina and Naomi would be sucked into the vortex!

Willa really, really wanted to warn her friends. But she kept her mouth firmly shut. It had taken a lot of effort to get that tear. She couldn't lose it now!

The shadowy whirlpool was getting closer to Azmina and Naomi. It was moving so quickly, there was nothing Willa could do. Fear gripped her as she watched her friends be overwhelmed by the swirling Shadow Sprites. She saw the surprise on their faces as they were spun around and down towards the depths of the river.

Willa shook off the fear that was slowing her down. She was *not* going to watch her friends be sucked into the vortex! She felt energy ripple through her body, restoring her tired muscles.

Willa started swimming harder and faster

than she ever had before. She had to get to her

friends. She had to save them!

With an extra-hard swish of her tail, Willa

dived into the seething mass. It was cold and

dark and scary. She heard the whispering

doubt. *You can't help your friends. You're too*

scared...

Willa froze. The Shadow Sprites were right: she *was* scared. *But it's not true that I can't do it*, Willa told herself firmly.

She could just make out Naomi and Azmina being whisked around like clothes in a washing machine. She reached out a paw to each of her friends.

She couldn't say anything with her mouth, so she let her eyes do the talking. *Hold on. I've got this.*

Naomi grabbed one paw as she whipped past, and Azmina the other. The whirlpool was so strong, Willa, too, was quickly picked up and whooshed around.

Willa was feeling dizzy, but she gathered

her strength and whipped her tail through the writing Shadow Sprites, sending them shooting off in all directions. Then, kicking with more power than she knew she had, Willa zoomed her friends up through the eye of the tornado and towards the surface.

The three exhausted Glitter Dragon Girls

broke the water's surface, gasping as they pulled themselves on to the riverbank.

"That was intense!" spluttered Naomi. "Willa, I have no idea how you managed to save us."

"Neither do I," said Azmina, taking great gulps of air. "You're incredible!"

But Willa couldn't join the conversation. She still had a mouthful of water! Very carefully, she opened her mouth and let out the water. A silver teardrop fell on to the grass.

Willa quickly scooped it up and put it into the magic apple. The sea-donkey tear sank into the potion and disappeared. She frowned. Nothing seemed to have happened. Maybe they needed more than one tear?

But then the potion began to roil and splutter. Willa clamped the lid back on to stop the potion from spilling over. One tear was definitely enough!

A moment later, Willa opened up the apple and peeked inside. The bubbles had settled down now and the potion was gently fizzing. The smell wafting up from it was a little like peppermint and a little like the ocean.

Feeling pleased, Willa turned to the others. "Phew. That was close! Now, let's get working on the last ingredient. What was it the Tree

Queen said? Something *invisible*, from somewhere deep. I guess that means deep in the river, right?"

Her heart sank a little. It wasn't much information to go on. Her heart sank even further when she looked at her friends.

"I can't go back into the water just yet," said Azmina, shaking her head. "That was scary and difficult. I need to get my strength back."

Naomi nodded. "Me too. I don't scare easily, but that was freaky! And I love swimming, but it's way more tiring than flying."

Willa was surprised. She felt the exact opposite!

"But we don't have time for a break," Willa

pointed out. "Did you see all those Shadow Sprites down there? If we don't make this potion soon, the whole river will be grey."

Azmina looked at her. "Maybe you should go ahead while we take a rest? You're such a great swimmer, but I'm not."

Willa looked at her friends in dismay. "But we're a team! We need to do this together."

"We are a team," agreed Naomi, still breathing heavily, "and we'll join you as soon as we can. But right now, Azmina and I will just hold you back."

Willa hated to admit it, but they were right. She could see how tired her friends were. She didn't want to do this alone, especially as it

was the hardest part! But she thought about how frightening it was watching her friends being sucked into that shadowy vortex. She had saved them this time. But she might not be so lucky next time.

She stood up, tucking the apple back into her

bag. "OK," she said, trying to keep the wobble out of her voice. "I'll go alone for now."

Naomi put her paw on Willa's. "We won't be far behind you. No matter how tired we are. Right, Azmina?"

"Of course!" agreed Azmina, nodding vigorously.

Willa smiled, feeling a little better. All the same, as she dived back into the river, she wished she had someone to keep her company.

7

Was it Willa's imagination, or was the river even greyer now than before? It felt colder too. The chill seeped into Willa, filling her with doubt.

"I don't think I can do this," she whispered to herself. As she spoke, she felt something beside her, radiating warmth and light.

"Of course you can!"

"Delphina!" Willa cried. "You're here!"

"As if I'd let you do this alone," chattered the silver dolphin in her funny squeaky voice.  "There are all kinds of weird creatures in this river. Whistling prawns, blinking strobe fish. Oh, and don't get too close to the scissor fish. They are very snippy."

Willa wrapped a wing around the dolphin and squeezed. "I'm so glad you're here," she said.

The quest suddenly felt a whole lot less scary.

Together, Willa and Delphina dived down,

down, down into the water. It must have been the deepest river in the world! The deeper they went, the darker the water became. But Delphina's silvery skin glowed, creating a warm cocoon of light.

All the same, Willa could only see a tail's length in any direction. Things kept brushing against her. But that was the least of Willa's problems. The real issue was that she had no idea what she was looking for!

"Did the Tree Queen give you any hints at all?" asked Delphina.

"She just said it came from somewhere deep, and that it was invisible," replied Willa. "But everything down here is invisible."

Even worse, Willa wasn't sure the ingredient was in the river at all. It might be in a deep hole somewhere. Willa felt her worries swell. Collecting something, when she had no idea what it was or where it was, felt...impossible.

They were so deep now that Willa could see the long, leafy weeds growing on the bottom of the river, rippling back and forth.

"Watch out!" called Delphina suddenly.

But it was too late. Willa crashed into a large fish swimming towards them. "Oh, I'm sorry—" she said, but the fish snapped its sharp silver teeth at her and swished off.

"A scissor fish!" said Delphina, swimming over. "Are you OK?"

"I'm fine," said Willa, but as she spoke, she felt something tumble out of her bag. The magic apple!

"There's a huge hole in your bag," groaned Delphina. "That scissor fish must have cut it as it went by."

There wasn't a moment to lose. If the magic apple fell into the river weeds, it would be very difficult to find in the dark. Willa pressed her wings against her side and swooped after the apple. Just as it was about to disappear into the weeds, she scooped it up with her wing. Yes!

"Good work, Willa!" cheered Delphina. "Now, let's get away from here. It's creepy."

Willa was about to agree when something

brushed against her paw. *Just a strand of river weed*, Willa told herself, swimming back to Delphina. But then another weed pressed against her.

Looking down, Willa saw a dark tendril reach up and wind itself around her leg. Hang on, weeds didn't do that! Her heart pounded.

So many mistakes. The Tree Queen will be disappointed in you, whispered the Shadow Sprites.

Willa tried to ignore the awful whispers. "Delphina!" she yelled. "There are Shadow Sprites hiding in the weeds!"

A Shadow Sprite was already wrapping itself around Delphina's tail. But the dolphin whipped around, using her sharp little teeth to nip it off.

Willa tried to pull away, but more and more Shadow Sprites were reaching for her. Their mean whispers came thick and fast. *You're all alone down here. Your friends left you. You don't belong on the Glitter Dragon team...*

"Stay away, Delphina!" Willa begged as she fought off the Shadow Sprites. "I don't want you to get caught. Swim to safety."

"There's no way I am leaving you," said the dolphin calmly, and she charged at the shadowy forms, biting them off. But no sooner

was Willa untangled from one than another would take hold. They seemed to be getting stronger. Soon Willa was completely tangled up in the shadowy weeds.

Willa looked around, feeling helpless. Maybe the Shadow Sprites were right. Maybe she would fail. Maybe she didn't belong on the team.

Then the Tree Queen's words came back to her. *I believe in you, Willa. You should too.*

Suddenly, even though the queen was not there, her words drowned out the doubt. The Tree Queen thought she could do this. *If she thinks I can, then I can!* Willa decided.

A rumbling began to build inside her. There was no way she was going to let the Shadow

Sprites beat her. She was going to find the last ingredient, no matter what!

The feeling was so big that she just had to let it out. *ROAR!*

The sound burst out of her, filling the water with dazzling swirls of silver and enormous bubbles, which floated off towards the surface.

"You're roaring the shadows away!" chattered Delphina. "Look!"

Sure enough, some of the Shadow Sprites had let go. With one more tremendous roar, the remaining Shadow Sprites fell away. Willa was free, thanks to her own magical roar!

But as she and Delphina quickly swam away, her good feelings began to fade. She was no closer to finding the potion's last ingredient. And the roaring had used up her remaining air. She wasn't sure she had enough to get herself to the surface!

Delphina swam along beside Willa as they headed up. She looked at Willa anxiously. "Are you OK?"

Willa shook her head. She was almost out of breath, and the surface looked like it was a long, long way away.

"Wait here," instructed the dolphin. "I'll get help."

Willa hated to see her little companion swimming off, but she had no choice. She needed air. Delphina had only been gone for a few moments when Willa saw her heading back down towards her.

Willa's heart skipped a beat. Following close behind Delphina were two shapes. *Could it be...? Yes! It was Azmina and Naomi!*

Her friends were swimming towards her, huge grins on their faces. They were wearing what looked like diving helmets. Azmina had an extra helmet tucked under each arm.

"That was so fast, Delphina!" Willa whispered,

almost out of breath entirely.

"They were already on their way down," chattered the dolphin happily.

"Here, put this on," instructed Azmina, holding out one of the strange helmet things. "It's full of air."

Willa took the object cautiously. It looked like a large fishbowl. But this was no fishbowl – it was soft and strangely squishy to the touch!

"How do I put it on?" she asked.

"You just pull it over your head," explained Naomi.

Willa did so, and gratefully gulped in the fresh air. "What are these things we're wearing?" she asked. "And where did you find them?"

"Don't you recognize them?" Azmina grinned. "They're bubbles from your magic roar!"

"We were on our way down to find you," explained Naomi, "when we heard you roar. We figured something bad must have happened. We were so worried!"

"But then," said Azmina, "these huge, silvery bubbles starting floating by. We knew right away that they came from you. They were still echoing your roar."

"One got stuck on my head," Azmina laughed. "Before I could pull it off, I realized

I could breathe with it on. My ears stopped hurting too."

"My roar made these?" Willa marvelled. "Amazing!"

"Have you found the last ingredient?" asked Naomi.

Willa made a face. "No. Maybe we should look somewhere else." But where? The river was long and deep.

Just then, Willa noticed that Azmina was looking at her strangely. *She thinks I've let them down*, she thought. Willa felt awful.

But Azmina was pointing over Willa's shoulder, her eyes very wide. "Um, guys? What is that?"

Willa and Naomi turned to look. Willa gave a yelp of surprise. Floating, right there, was an enormous squid! Its tentacles were as thick as pythons. Its eyes were the size of car wheels, and they were fixed on the Glitter Dragons.

"It's a giant squid!" Willa stage-whispered.

"Giant is the word," Naomi whispered back.

The huge squid began to move slowly towards them, its tentacles outstretched.

"There's no way we can outswim that thing. Can we roar it away?" whispered Azmina.

"Let's try. One, two, three!" called Willa.

Together, the Dragon Girls roared. But they'd forgotten they had bubble helmets on! Their helmets filled with swirling glitter.

Willa felt like she was trapped inside a snow globe.

The giant squid gave a yelp and released a squirt of silvery ink into the water.

"Argh! It's attacking us!" Azmina cried. The Dragon Girls grabbed paws and moved back.

"Argh! You're scary!" wailed the squid at the same time.

That was a funny thing for a giant squid to say. Willa looked closely. Was the squid... *trembling*?

"I thought you'd help me find Mummy. But you're meeeeeeeeean."

"Oh, you're just a little kid!" Willa cooed. She instantly forgot her fear, swam over and put a wing around the creature. "Are you lost?"

Delphina swam over and gave the squid a friendly nose poke.

"Yes!" the squid sobbed, patting Delphina and staring up at Willa. "I was swimming with Mummy, but the shadows came and then I couldn't see her any more."

"We'll help you find your mum," said Willa,

thinking of the time she'd lost her own mum at the museum.

"If this is a kid, I can't wait to see the mother." Naomi grinned.

She didn't have long to wait. No sooner had Naomi spoken than the water around them began to churn and fill with tumbling bubbles.

"What's happening?" Azmina gulped.

From the deep, another squid came into view. It made the first squid look like a bath toy.

"Mummy!" the kid squid wailed, rushing over and flinging his tentacles around her.

"Oh, my baby!" the mother squid cried, stroking her son with a tentacle the size of an oak tree. "I just hate this shadow water! It's

making me feel dizzy, and I couldn't find you.
Then when I heard roaring, I was so worried
you were in danger." The mum squid turned
her huge eyes suspiciously on the Dragon Girls.
"Are you in danger?"

"No, these dragons are nice," said the kid
squid, to everyone's relief.

However, the mother squid did not seem

convinced. She pointed a tentacle at the silvery ink that was still swirling around in the shadow-darkened water.

"But you squirted your invisible ink," she said to her child. "You only do that when you're scared."

"I was scared at first," explained the squid kid. "These dragons are so big. And their roars are very loud. But then I realized they were nice."

"You think we're big?" Azmina laughed. "Isn't that funny, Willa?"

But Willa wasn't listening. "Did you say *invisible ink*?" she asked the squid mum.

"Yes," said the enormous creature proudly. "We're invisible-ink squid. Very rare. Normally, you can't see our ink. It's only because of this horrible shadowy water that it's visible."

Willa turned in triumph to Azmina and Naomi. "Invisible squid ink is the last ingredient!"

9

"Azmina, pass me a bubble!" urged Willa. Then she turned to the squid mum. "Do you mind if we use your special ink to make our potion?"

"Anything to stop those Shadow Sprites!" said the squid mum.

The squid kid puffed out his chest in pride.

Azmina handed her the last bubble that she

had tucked away under her wing. Willa passed it carefully through a swirl of invisible ink and the silvery liquid seeped into the centre of the bubble, leaving the river water behind. She had clearly roared out a very special bubble! Willa felt triumphant for a moment.

Then she saw that most of the water around them was almost completely grey.

"Come on! Let's get to the surface," she said to the others.

"Do you have time for a cup of sea-squirt tea?" asked the mum, lifting a tentacle like a pinkie finger.

"Stay for tea!" the kid squid yelled, clapping

his tentacles in excitement. "And I can show you what a good tickler I am."

"Thanks, but we must make this potion as soon as possible," said Willa politely.

It was nice to get the invitation, but she did NOT fancy being tickled by a giant squid. She could tell from the faces of the other two Dragon Girls that neither did they!

"Well, drop by any time," said the mum squid.

She and her son waved all their arms and tentacles goodbye.

Willa and her friends swam towards the surface. It was a bit awkward for Willa, carrying the bubble of invisible ink under one wing. Luckily, swimming up was easier than swimming down, and before long, the Dragon Girls broke through the water's surface.

Immediately, their bubble helmets popped and they could breathe in the crisp Magic Forest air again.

"Willa! Be careful the bubble with the ink doesn't pop too!" warned Naomi.

With a guilty jump, Willa looked down at the bubble. Phew! It was still in one piece. In fact, the bubble's surface had hardened in the air. It now felt like delicate glass. Carefully, Willa flew out of the water, sending a shower of silvery drops into the air.

She landed on the riverbank. Azmina and Naomi landed beside her.

"Here goes," said Willa, pulling the apple out of the bag, which had magically repaired itself after the scissor fish incident. She opened the apple and held the bubble over the apple. It was too big to drop inside. "Should I break it?" she wondered, but as she spoke, the bubble shattered into a thousand pieces. She groaned. "What's happened to the ink?"

She couldn't see it anywhere.

"Maybe it's become invisible again now that we're out of the shadow water?" suggested Naomi.

"Maybe. But where is it?" wondered Willa.

Azmina pointed at the potion. "Hopefully in there!"

The three dragons peered into the apple. Within it bubbled a beautiful liquid, the colour of a moonlit ocean.

"Do you think it's right?" asked Willa, a little anxiously.

"It's perfect," declared Naomi. "You can tell just by looking at it."

"I think so too." Azmina nodded. "But what do we do with it?"

"We need to get it into the waterways of the Magic Forest," decided Willa. "Maybe we could pour it into the top of the waterfall?"

"Great idea!" Azmina and Naomi chorused.

Flying up the waterfall wasn't quite as fun as sliding down it had been. The spray beat down on them, and the grey water stung their eyes. But Willa was full of energy. She couldn't wait to see if the potion worked!

Soon, the Dragon Girls were hovering above the mighty waterfall. Willa held the apple tightly between her paws.

"So, should we just pour it out into the waterfall?" asked Azmina.

Willa frowned, thinking hard. It had seemed like a good idea before, but now she wasn't so sure. If they just dropped the potion into the water, it might stay in one big gloop and not spread out. They needed to find a way to sprinkle the potion as widely as possible.

She could think of one way. But was it too wild?

Naomi examined her face. "You have an idea, don't you? I can tell from your face."

"Yes," admitted Willa. "But maybe it's silly..."

"Your ideas are never silly," said Azmina firmly.

"Yeah, we Glitter Dragon Girls are as filled with good ideas as we are glitter!" Naomi laughed.

Willa laughed too. "Actually, my idea is about our glitter. I was thinking, maybe we roar out a glitter cloud and fill it with the potion. Then the cloud can rain the potion down over the water."

Willa looked at Azmina and Naomi a little nervously. Would they like her idea?

Azmina did a mid-air flip. "I KNEW it would be a great idea!"

"Me too." Naomi grinned. "C'mon, let's roar!"

The three Dragon Girls each took a huge gulp of air. Then they roared out the biggest roars they could. Silver, gold, and rainbow-coloured glitter swirled in the air. It was dazzling. The bright specks tumbled and whirled over one another, forming a sparkling cloud.

"Keep going!" called Willa. "Let's make it even bigger."

The Dragon Girls roared and roared until an enormous glitter cloud hung in the air.

"I am all out of roar," croaked Azmina. "Is it big enough yet?"

Willa nodded. "I think so. I'll add the potion."

Willa flew up above the cloud, pouring the

silvery potion over it. Then she flew back to the others. She really hoped this would work!

For a moment, the cloud did nothing at all. And then very fine silvery drops began to fall like enchanted rain.

"It's working! It's working!" Azmina cried in delight.

Willa held her breath as the first drops landed in the waterfall. The water was so bubbly it was impossible to see if it had changed colour at all.

But then Naomi called out, "Look!"

Willa saw bedraggled Shadow Sprites crawling out of the water and slithering into the forest. They looked tired and heavy, like wet towels being dragged along the ground.

She turned to look at the river. What she saw made her flap her wings with joy. Thin streaks of silver were moving fast through the grey water, restoring its bright and magical colour.

"We did it!" yelled Willa. "Glitter Dragon Girls, shine on!"

10

Willa felt something press against her side. It was Delphina.

"It's time to head back to the glade," the dolphin chattered. "The Tree Queen wants to see you all."

The Glitter Dragon Girls began flying back the way they had come, following the course of the river. Looking down, Willa could see the effects of their potion. Ribbons of blue curled through the grey water. The river was quickly turning back to its dazzling blue.

Azmina and Naomi flew on either side of her.

"Willa, I know you didn't think you could lead this quest. But you did a great job," said Azmina.

"Thanks to you, the forest is looking beautiful again," added Naomi.

Willa felt a surge of happiness at her friends' kind words. The forest did look great, but Willa was pretty sure they hadn't seen the last of the Shadow Sprites.

A light wind began to blow, and suddenly Willa made a very cool discovery.

"Hey, guys! We can surf the wind!" Willa yelled.

She showed her friends how to catch an air current and glide along on top of it, like riding a wave at the beach.

Azmina and Naomi both tried it, but they couldn't do it nearly as well.

"You make it look easy!" Azmina laughed. "I keep ending up upside down!"

"We'll practise more next time," promised Willa. "Look, there's the glade."

Sure enough, down below was the glowing

heart of the Magic Forest, the Tree Queen standing tall at its centre. Together, the Glitter Dragons zoomed down.

They passed through the protective shield and landed on the soft, mint-green grass.

"Well done, Glitter Dragons!" said the Tree Queen.

The queen's voice was much stronger. And Willa saw the sparkle had returned to her warm brown eyes. The shine was back in her flowing hair. Her limbs looked even stronger than before.

"You look wonderful," she blurted without thinking.

Was it rude to comment on a queen's appearance? Willa wasn't sure.

But the Tree Queen smiled. "I heard on the wind that you had completed your quest. But I already knew. The water seeping through my roots is so much cleaner. I am feeling much better. Congratulations, Dragon Girls. Especially you, Willa."

If dragons could blush, Willa's face would have been bright red. "Thanks, but it was really a team thing."

The Tree Queen nodded. "I know. I am very happy with how you've come together as a group."

The Glitter Dragon Girls grinned at one another. There was nothing better than being praised by the Tree Queen!

"Do you have the apple?" asked the queen.

Willa pulled it from the bag. It was now withered and had lost its beautiful shine. As she passed the apple to the Tree Queen, it dissolved into a tiny shower of raindrops.

They sparkled like diamonds for a moment, then – *pop-pop-pop* – they disappeared.

"Do you need us to come back again?" asked Willa after she'd got over the shock of seeing an apple disappear before her very eyes.

The Tree Queen nodded, her face serious again. "Yes, I will need you again very soon. What do you think, Dragon Girls? Are you up for one last quest?"

Willa, Azmina, and Naomi didn't need to look at one another to know they all felt the same. Of course they were! The quests definitely had some tricky moments, but nothing felt better than helping the Magic Forest.

The Tree Queen rewarded them with her warm smile. "I thought you would. Now, find your travel charm to focus on and return to your homes the way you came."

Willa looked around, knowing her special shell would be somewhere nearby. Yes! There it lay, not far from the Tree Queen's mossy green robes. She scooped it up and turned to her friends to say goodbye. "See you at school tomorrow!"

Then, holding the shell tightly in her paw, she flew back through the force field. She followed the curve of the river until she arrived at the spot where she'd entered the Magic Forest. The water was now a brilliant aqua.

Willa tossed the shell into the lake and watched it gently sink to the bottom. Then she began to chant.

Magic Forest, Magic Forest, come explore.
Magic Forest, Magic Forest, hear my roar!

As the words left her mouth, Willa dived into the lake. Small bubbles tickled her sides as she swam, smooth and strong, towards the shell.

A school of chic black-and-white fish darted by. "Thanks for making the water sweet again!" they called in unison.

"No problem!" Willa smiled.

As Willa swam towards her special shell, things began to change. The river creatures faded from view. The waving water plants disappeared. By the time Willa reached for the shell, the riverbed had become familiar blue tiles.

Willa swam up until she broke the surface. Her coach, Nancy, finished her phone call and turned around.

"Willa! Are you STILL in there?" Nancy slipped her phone into her pocket and crossed her arms. She had a half-annoyed, half-amused

expression on her face. "I swear you would live underwater if you could!"

Willa swam to the edge and jumped out. "Sorry!" She grinned at her coach. "I got carried away."

"It's great that you spend so much time at the pool," said Nancy, passing Willa her towel, "but it's important to visit other places too."

"Oh, don't worry," called Willa as she headed off to the changing rooms. "I visit plenty of other places!"

If only Nancy knew!

Read Naomi's adventure next!

Naomi loves being a Glitter Dragon Girl. She can fly above treetops and roar glittery bursts of magic. Best of all, she and the other Glitter Dragons are keeping their beloved Magic Forest safe from the Shadow Sprites.

But all is not as it seems in this special place. The Shadow Sprites' power is growing . . . and they may not be alone. Naomi must harness all the dragon magic she's learned so far to lead the Glitter Dragon Girls against this new threat.

ABOUT THE AUTHORS

Maddy Mara is the pen name of Australian creative duo Hilary Rogers and Meredith Badger. Hilary and Meredith have been collaborating on books for children for nearly two decades.

Hilary is an author and former publishing director, who has created several series that have sold into the millions. Meredith is the author of countless books for kids and young adults, and also teaches English as a foreign language to children.

The Dragon Girls is their first time co-writing under the name Maddy Mara, the melding of their respective daughters' names.